Beast Quest®

KROKOL
THE FATHER
OF FEAR

BY ADAM BLADE

ORCHARD

With special thanks to Conrad Mason

For Joshua Simpson

www.beastquest.co.uk

ORCHARD BOOKS

First published in Great Britain in 2020 by The Watts Publishing Group

1 3 5 7 9 10 8 6 4 2

Text © 2020 Beast Quest Limited.
Cover and inside illustrations by Steve Sims
© Beast Quest Limited 2020

Beast Quest is a registered trademark of Beast Quest Limited
Series created by Beast Quest Limited, London

A CIP catalogue record for this book is available from the British Library.

ISBN 978 1 40835 781 1

Printed in Great Britain

The paper and board used in this book are made from wood from responsible sources

Orchard Books
An imprint of Hachette Children's Group
Part of The Watts Publishing Group Limited
Carmelite House, 50 Victoria Embankment, London EC4Y 0DZ

An Hachette UK Company
www.hachette.co.uk
www.hachettechildrens.co.uk

Welcome to the world of Beast Quest!

Tom was once an ordinary village boy, until he travelled to the City, met King Hugo and discovered his destiny. Now he is the Master of the Beasts, sworn to defend Avantia and its people against Evil. Tom draws on the might of the magical Golden Armour, and is protected by powerful tokens granted to him by the Good Beasts of Avantia. Tom and his loyal companion Elenna are always ready to visit new lands and tackle the enemies of the realm.

While there's blood in his veins, Tom will never give up the Quest…

There are special gold coins to collect in this book. You will earn one coin for every chapter you read.

Find out what to do with your coins at the end of the book.

CONTENTS

Banners fly from the walls of King Hugo's Palace and all Avantia rejoices at Tom's latest victory. The people worship the snivelling wretch as if he's their saviour.

Well, forgive me if I'm not bowing down. He killed my father Sanpao and drove my mother Kensa from the kingdom.

So, in revenge, I'm going to spoil their little party.

Soon Avantia will face a Beast like no other.

And when they look for their little hero to save their skins, he will be nowhere to be found.

Ria

A DARK PATH

"There it is!" cried Daltec. "The Great Palace of Pyloris!"

"Or what's left of it," muttered Elenna.

The journey from the forest of Morax had been long and slow, across sweeping plains, but Elenna resisted the urge to rest. A wide stone path stretched ahead, leading

straight through overgrown gardens
to the palace.

Once, the Great Palace of Pyloris
must have been white. But now the
stones were dirty and crumbling,
and the high walls were covered

in creeping green vines. The great
golden domes on each tower had
turned dull with neglect.

Under the grey sky, the air was
chill. Elenna couldn't help shivering.
It's so quiet here...

"It looks completely abandoned," said Daltec.

Elenna shook her head. "I'm not so sure." She unhooked the compass from her belt and checked the black needle, which wobbled to aim right at the palace. The needle was made from the same metal as Tom's armour, now under an Evil enchantment, and it always pointed straight to him. "Tom's in there," she said. "So we'd better take a closer look."

We've got to find him, Elenna reminded herself.

As they passed a pair of dried-up old fountains, Elenna couldn't shake off an uneasy feeling. There was no sign of life here. Not even a twittering of birdsong.

Ahead, a row of stone soldiers stood guard on either side of the path, like sentries on duty. Their faces were worn away by time, and most of their spears had broken off entirely.

Daltec was panting, struggling to keep up. "Be careful!" he said. "We don't know what might be waiting for us in there."

Elenna shook her head. "Maybe not...but there aren't any Beasts left, right? It's like you said. Long ago, Krokol, the Father of Fear, was split into three parts. We've already defeated Electro, Fluger and Morax.

So now we just need to rescue Tom from Ria."

"I suppose you're right," said Daltec. But his eyes darted anxiously from side to side.

They skirted round an ornamental pool, the water green and stagnant. At last they arrived at the entrance, and Elenna looked up in awe. The archway was twice as tall as Daltec. The golden gates stood open, each door as thick as a tree trunk.

"It must have been incredible once," Elenna whispered. Even more incredible than King Hugo's castle back home!

Daltec nodded. "Oh yes. Pyloris was the heart of an empire! Home to powerful magic, astonishing science and wondrous culture."

"So what happened?" asked Elenna.

Daltec looked stern. "Greed," he said. "The last King of Pyloris was never satisfied. He wanted to know more and more… And his quest for knowledge led him down a dark path, to an evil magic that he couldn't control."

Elenna tightened her grip on her bow. "Come on – let's find Tom and get out of here. I don't like this place one bit."

Their footsteps echoed through a long, cavernous hall. At the end of it, they stepped through another archway into a huge chamber. Tattered tapestries hung on the walls, and at the end of the room was a dais with a large, white stone throne on it. The chamber was cold, still and silent. *It's like King Hugo's Great Hall*, thought Elenna. *Except bigger...and creepier!*

Then she saw something else. Beneath each faded tapestry was a large marble chest – and one of them, halfway down the length of the chamber, was open.

Elenna crossed the hall to peer inside. She frowned. There was no treasure there – just a heap of parchment, pale purple in colour and covered in black writing. The ink glistened as though it had only just flowed from a quill.

"The Scrolls of the Living Past," breathed Daltec, his voice full of awe. "Aduro once told me of them. They're written in magical ink that never

dries! And if you touch it, the scroll will reveal the history of Pyloris."

Carefully, Elenna lifted a page from the chest. Right in the middle of the parchment, the ink was smudged with a fingerprint. "Someone touched it recently," she said. "I'd bet anything it was Ria!"

"But why?" wondered Daltec.

Elenna shrugged. "There's only one way to find out."

She laid her finger on the smudged ink, and at once, the room began to spin.

Elenna stumbled. She felt dizzy. *What's happening?* The room was flashing past them, the walls and the tapestries whirling faster and faster.

Then suddenly, it stopped.

She blinked. *Everything's different!*
Gazing round in astonishment, she
saw a rich red carpet lying across the
floor. The walls were gleaming white,
and the tapestries were whole again
and brightly coloured.

"It's the past!" whispered Daltec.
"This is what the throne room used
to look like. We're actually seeing it
for ourselves!"

Gazing round, Elenna felt her
stomach lurch. Sitting on the throne
was a tall, thin man in a white
linen robe, with a thick silver band
around his brow. He was gazing
right through Elenna, as though he
couldn't see her. *Of course he can't,*

she reminded herself. *This is just a magical vision!*

"That must be King Jorah," said Daltec. "The last King of Pyloris."

King Jorah looked down, and Elenna saw that he held something in his hands. It was a crystal goblet, filled almost to the brim with a thick black liquid.

"What is that?" asked Elenna. But Daltec was just staring, with a look of horror on his face.

As they watched, King Jorah lifted the goblet to his lips. He closed his eyes, hesitating for just a moment. Then he drank.

"No…" whispered Daltec.

At once, the king's eyes snapped

open. Elenna gasped – they had turned utterly black. His mouth opened in a silent scream. Then he jerked forward, tumbling to the ground. The goblet clattered off the dais and smashed into a thousand crystal shards.

Elenna lunged forward to help, but Daltec held her back. "There's nothing you can do," he said. "This has already happened."

The king doubled up, writhing on the floor. Black smoke rose from his body, filling the room and hiding him from view. When it finally cleared, Elenna saw the king stagger to his feet.

Her flesh crawled. King Jorah

was…different. He stood twice as tall as before, and was still growing. He was even thinner and more skeletal, and his skin had turned the colour of ash. Hooked talons stuck out from his feet, and his fingers were too long, curving monstrously.

He's a Beast! thought Elenna.

The creature reached up, long fingers exploring his own new, terrible face. His features were sunken, his eyes jet black. His teeth were rotten yellow shards. He threw back his head and let out a whooping howl of triumph.

Elenna's hand closed on an arrow shaft. "What is this?" she said.

"The truth," said Daltec, grimly.

"I understand now... King Jorah didn't summon Krokol, the Father of Fear. He *became* him! So when Tanner ventured to the kingdom and

managed to split Krokol into three separate Beasts, Jorah was lost for ever. The kingdom had no leader and fell into ruin."

Elenna frowned as a dark thought struck her. "Is this why Ria came here and used Tom to defeat the three Beasts?" she wondered. "You don't think she's planning to bring Krokol back somehow...do you?"

KROKOL STIRS

"Is it time, mistress?" asked Tom.

Torches flickered on the walls, throwing strange shadows across the flagstones of the dungeons. Tom crouched in a cell, watching Ria at work. The pirate girl had built a fire in the middle of the floor and set a golden pot over it.

Ria smiled, her mohawk glowing

blood-red in the firelight. "Not long now," she said. She tossed Electro's shining feather into the pot, then Fluger's scale. Morax's tooth went in last – all the tokens Tom had

collected on his recent Quests in
Pyloris. A hissing sound filled the
cell, and black smoke coiled up
from inside the pot. "Once the three
tokens are combined, Krokol will
return," said Ria. "And best of all,
no one can stop us! Least of all
that pathetic girl Elenna, and her
useless wizard friend."

"It's a brilliant plan!" said Tom.
Or is it...? He knew that Ria was
his mistress, and of course she
knew best. But something was
bothering him.

"There's just one thing," Tom
said carefully. "Do you really want
to summon a Beast? It sounds
dangerous."

"Dangerous for the Avantians!"
cackled Ria. "Don't you worry, Tom. I
have a feeling I'll be just fine. Krokol
will make me even more powerful.
Then you and I will return to
Avantia...and destroy the kingdom!"

"Good idea," said Tom, nodding
eagerly. "It's just...I've seen people
try to control Beasts before. It never
goes well."

Ria couldn't stop grinning. "Oh,
I think this will go very well." She
gestured to the pot. "Come and see."

Tom leaned over it to peer inside.
Something strange was happening
to the Beast tokens. They seemed to
be melting, dissolving into a thick
black goo that coated the bottom of

the pot. Tom's eyes stung, and his nostrils burned with the foul stench of it. *It's like swamp water mixed with pig's muck...*

Ria drew a jewelled dagger and dipped its blade into the pot, stirring all three tokens until the gloop was well mixed together.

"Now give me your magic jewel," she said, holding out a hand. "The red one."

Tom felt a prickling at the back of his neck. "Torgor's ruby? What do you need that for?" he asked.

Ria snorted. "Don't be stupid! How else will I be able to communicate with Krokol? I must make sure the Beast trusts me, right from the start."

Reluctantly, Tom reached for his belt, plucking the jewel. "I suppose that makes sense," he said.

He was just passing Ria the jewel, when she snatched hold of his wrist. *Swish!* Her dagger flicked across the back of his hand. Tom gasped at the sudden, unexpected pain.

When he looked down, he saw that the cut was black, not red. His eyes darted to Ria's dagger. It was smoking, the blade coated in the black gloop from inside the pot.

"What have you done, mistress?" he asked.

Ria just sneered at him. Then

she snatched the jewel and kicked him hard in the chest. Tom tumbled over backwards, caught off balance. Before he could get to his feet, Ria kicked over the pot and tripod and darted out of the cell.

Clang! She slammed the door shut and turned the key.

"Goodbye, Tom," she said. "The next time I see you, I have a feeling you won't be quite yourself!" She turned, laughing, and strode away.

"Mistress!" Tom called after her. "I don't understand!"

Then he gasped. Suddenly his blood turned to fire, flowing through his veins right to the tips of his fingers and toes. He began

to shudder. He felt as though
something was inside him, shaking
his whole body.

Something that was trying to get out...

What's happening to me?

3

A SECRET PASSAGE

Elenna could see straight through the image of Krokol now. *The enchantment is fading*, she realised.

A moment later, the vision was gone entirely, and she and Daltec stood alone again in the ruined throne room. She shivered, trying not to think about the terrifying Beast she had just seen.

She tossed the parchment back into the chest. Then she noticed something. On the dusty stone floor nearby, there was a trail of footprints. *No...two trails.*

"Do you think...?" said Daltec.

"Tom and Ria must be close!" finished Elenna.

Holding her breath, she followed the footprints across the stone floor, straight to the throne. There they stopped. "They must have come this way," she murmured.

"But where did they go next?" wondered Daltec.

"They can't have just vanished." Elenna examined the throne. It was made of solid white stone, just like the dais it stood on. *Impossible to move*, thought Elenna. *Unless…*

She ran her hands over the top of the armrests, then under them. *There!* She felt something. A nub of stone, which gave way when she pulled it, like a lever.

"Look out!" gasped Daltec.

Elenna's heart lurched. The whole dais was moving, sliding smoothly to one side and taking them with it. Beneath, a square opening was revealed. White stone steps led down from it, disappearing into darkness.

Daltec sighed, looking pale. "We're going to have to go down there, aren't we?"

Elenna nodded grimly. "I'm afraid so."

She led the way, moving slowly and carefully as they descended. Daltec hitched up his robe and followed.

The steps were worn and chipped, and chunks of broken stone lay in their path. *No one's been this way in centuries!* thought Elenna. *Well – almost no one...*

At last they reached the bottom of the steps. As her eyes got used to the dark, Elenna saw the dim form of a corridor stretching ahead. She quietly drew an arrow and fitted it to her bow. "Can you hear anything?" she whispered.

"Nothing," said Daltec. She could only just see the wizard's eyes glinting in the dark.

As quietly as she could, Elenna tiptoed down the corridor. Her fingers rested on her bow, ready for action.

The corridor curved round, and the walls glowed orange up ahead, as though lit by torches.

Suddenly Daltec cried out. Elenna whirled round, raising her bow.

"Sorry!" said the wizard, sounding a little embarrassed. "I just tripped on something."

Peering down, Elenna spotted a shard of metal on the ground. It was flat and dull with age, but she could tell it had once been part of a blade.

"Look!" said Daltec. He pointed to another, larger shard of metal close by. "It's a sword blade. It must have broken in battle."

Elenna knelt to look closer. A swirling image was etched into the larger piece of metal. "It's some sort of bird," she said, frowning. "No…it's a phoenix!"

Daltec raised his eyebrows. "And not just any phoenix. That's Epos, faithful companion of Tanner."

"Avantia's first Master of the Beasts," said Elenna, in awe. "So this sword really is ancient! It must be the one Tanner used to fight Krokol."

"Right before he was defeated," said a voice from behind them.

Elenna spun round. Standing in the glow of the torchlight was a tall girl dressed in leather, with a cruel smile and a crest of blood-red hair. *Ria!*

Quick as a flash, Elenna had

her arrow pointed straight at the
pirate. Her fingers curled around the
bowstring…

"Not so fast!" sneered Ria, holding

up a hand. "Shoot me, and you can say goodbye to your dear friend Tom."

"What have you done with him?" snapped Elenna.

Ria chuckled. "You know, I'd hate to spoil the surprise."

A distant wailing drifted through the corridor, and Elenna's stomach twisted with unease. It sounded like the noise of an animal in terrible pain.

"What is that?" asked Daltec, his voice trembling.

"It's Tom, of course!" said Ria. "Why don't you go and say hello? I'm sure he'll be pleased to see you... *You* might not be pleased to see *him*, though!" She cackled horribly.

Heart racing, Elenna lowered her bow and ran down the corridor. She rounded the corner, heading past torches on the walls. Daltec's footsteps echoed behind her.

The corridor opened out into a dungeon with cells on either side. Elenna stopped, panting, staring all around.

There! She spotted Tom through a barred door, crouched in a corner of the cell. But her relief quickly turned to dread. He was hunched over and shivering, and she couldn't see his face. "Tom!" she called. "Are you all right?"

She crossed the floor and rattled

the door, but it was locked. Lowering her shoulder she threw herself against it, but the door held firm.

"Wait!" yelled Daltec.

Elenna took a step back.

Tom was jerking about now, his limbs flailing as he toppled to the flagstones. Elenna watched in horror as her friend's body began to pulse and swell. His skin was changing colour right in front of her eyes, an ash-grey stain spreading along each arm. His fingers curled like claws and gripped the floor.

He's changing, she realised, her hope draining away. *Just like King Jorah, in the vision. He's turning into a Beast!*

FATHER OF FEAR

Tom's whole body burned with pain.

He gasped for air, but he couldn't breathe. He felt as though his bones and ligaments were tearing apart. Glancing down, he saw his arms had changed. They bulged with muscle, and the flesh had taken on a corpse-like grey pallor. His nails thickened and grew before his eyes. Across his swelling chest and limbs, the black armour expanded like a second skin.

Tom opened his mouth to scream, but the voice that came out wasn't his. It was a howl that shook his chest. A howl of...triumph.

I'm...losing...control...

Tom gasped one last time.

Then he began to laugh. Because he wasn't Tom any more.

I am Krokol. Father of Fear.

Krokol reached out. He had to touch something, to prove he was real – that he had returned. He raked his black talons across the wall of the cell, and felt the stone give way. *It is true. I live!*

He snorted and ran his tongue over

his jagged teeth. It was time at last. Time for him to take his kingdom back once more.

Nearby, someone gasped in terror.

Krokol whirled round. There, gawping at him through the bars of the cell – a weak little girl, and a young man, no stronger, dressed in robes. *Behold Krokol, and weep!*

No bars could hold him. He took the metal door in his hands and tore it away with a screech. As he tossed it aside, the humans darted back to hide in the shadows.

Cowards! Not worthy to be my first victims.

Krokol stepped out of the cell. He remembered this palace well. Now it

was his to destroy as he pleased…

He prowled down the corridor, tearing down torches with his claws. The ceiling was too low, so he reached up and smashed a fist into it. The stone shuddered, but with a second

blow he broke right through. Rocks
and masonry rained down. As the dust
settled, Krokol stretched to take hold
of the floor above. He heaved himself
up into a corridor full of suits of
armour.

Krokol strode on, destroying the suits of armour one by one. Some he kicked to pieces. Others he hurled against the walls. His heart thundered with the joy of the hunt. He couldn't wait to spill his first drops of blood...

The door at the end of the corridor was too small for him, so Krokol hammered the wall with his fists instead, smashing it apart.

He stepped over the rubble, finding himself in a vast chamber with no ceiling. It must have fallen in, long ago. Above him, the sky was deep blue and studded with stars. Krokol knew it would have been beautiful to a human, but he didn't care whether he killed by night or day.

There was something familiar about the room. The slabs of green and white marble beneath his talons… The mirrors on the walls, mostly broken now and all covered in dust…

I remember. This was where he had fought the warrior Tanner. Everything looked so different now, as though centuries had passed since that day. His lip curled with fury. How could he have allowed such a feeble human to defeat him?

"Krokol!"

He started. The voice seemed to come from inside his head. He peered around and saw someone, a human girl with a crest of red hair. She had stepped out from behind him, as though she had been following. She clutched a red jewel in her fist, pulsing with magic.

"Krokol, you will obey me!" said the girl's voice, echoing through his head. "I brought you back. I, Ria, daughter of Kensa the sorceress and Sanpao the Pirate King! You are mine to command."

Krokol snorted with laughter. *Foolish little girl. I bow to no one!* He bent down and snatched hold of her. She struggled, squealing, but she was even more puny than she looked. Her arms were as brittle as tinder, ready to be snapped by his mighty claws...

"Tanner!" came the girl's voice. "Revenge!"

Krokol stopped. *What did you say?*

"Tanner defeated you, didn't he?"

she said quickly. "I can help you get revenge."

Even the warrior's name kindled a burning rage in Krokol's gut. He snarled at the little girl. *Tanner is dead.*

"But his kingdom lives on," said the girl's voice. "Avantia! The land he swore to protect. We can destroy it – together. The Avantians are our common enemy, Krokol. And I can open a gateway that will lead you there. Straight to the heart of Avantia."

Krokol hesitated. His fingers itched to pull the girl apart. But if what she said was true...if he could finally take revenge on the people of that pathetic warrior who had banished him for so long...

He relaxed his grip and allowed the girl to wriggle free. There would be time enough to kill her later.

After my revenge.

5

LIGHTNING PATH

Elenna crouched in the shadows,
waiting until the last echoes of
Krokol's rampaging footsteps had
died away.

As soon as it was safe, she ran
around the mangled cell door
and darted inside. She spotted
Tom's sword and shield, propped
up against a wall. Ria must have

told him to leave them there. She felt a stab of fury. Tom had done everything the pirate ordered him to do, and she had still betrayed him.

The thought of him trapped like that, in the body of the Beast, made her feel sick. *I'll get you out of this*, she swore. *Whatever it takes...*

"What are we going to do?" asked Daltec, emerging from his hiding place behind a barrel.

"What Tom and I always do," said Elenna. "Defeat the Beast!"

Daltec frowned. "But...this time, Tom *is* the Beast!"

"Our Tom is still in there, somewhere," said Elenna. "We just have to free him."

She slung Tom's shield on her back,
and slid the sword through her belt.
Then she led the way, running along
the corridor in the direction Krokol
had gone.

The Beast wasn't hard to follow. Burned-out torches lay here and there, metal brackets twisted and torn from the walls wherever Krokol had passed. And before long, they found a heap of rubble and a massive hole gaping in the ceiling.

Elenna climbed through to the floor above, then reached to lend Daltec a hand, as he scrambled up after her. Together they hurried on down the corridor. They passed bent and battered suits of armour, lying like dead bodies across the floor.

At the end of the corridor, the wall had been smashed to pieces. Elenna stepped through, and her breath caught in her throat.

There he is!

Krokol was facing away, bending down to place something on the floor. Elenna saw Ria step out from his fingers, brushing down her leather clothes. The pirate's gaze fell on Elenna, and she pointed, her lips curling into a sneer of triumph.

The Beast rose and turned. His cold eyes fixed on Elenna. They glittered with hunger, and he bared his rotten, yellow teeth.

Elenna's heart began to pound. There was something familiar about the Beast's face. As horrifying as it was, she could almost see the outline of Tom's features there.

Daltec stepped up next to her,

throwing his hands out. His fingers twitched, and an ice-blue light glowed around them for an instant…but it flickered and died.

"It's no use," gasped Daltec. The effort had left him panting, and his brow slick with sweat. "My magic doesn't work here!"

Krokol strode towards them. His black armour gleamed in the moonlight, and Elenna could feel the floor trembling with every step he took.

"Your bow!" cried Daltec. "Aduro's antidote is on the arrowheads, remember? If you can hit the Beast, perhaps it will break Ria's enchantment of Tom."

Elenna nodded. She reached for her quiver, but a chill settled in her heart when she realised that she had just two arrows left. If she missed, she'd only have one more chance.

And if she hit, even if it broke the spell...would Tom survive?

A mocking laugh rang out across the hall. Elenna saw Ria hovering at a doorway on the far side. She blew Elenna a kiss, then disappeared through the door.

Think fast, Elenna told herself.

But it was too late. Krokol broke into a charge. His pounding feet shook the floor so much that Elenna stumbled. And before she could manage to regain her footing, the

Beast brought his fist swinging down.

Elenna shoved Daltec to one side, just in time.

CRRRACK! The Beast's knuckles shattered the green marble slab

where the wizard had just been standing.

Krokol swept his other hand round, like a giant wiping crumbs from a table. Elenna tugged Daltec down, flattening both of them against the marble. She felt her hair ruffled as the Beast's hand passed just above her head.

"Tom!" she shouted, desperately. "It's me! It's Elenna!"

Krokol gave a howl that sounded almost like a laugh.

He's toying with us, Elenna realised, as she helped Daltec to his feet. Then, hands shaking, she drew one of the two arrows. Even if Tom had heard her from within

Krokol, he was still under Ria's enchantment. And the antidote on the arrows was the only way to break that spell.

She took aim, closing one eye and levelling the arrow. At the edge of Krokol's shoulder, there was a gap between the black armour plates. She pulled back, feeling the bowstring tighten...

"Do it, Elenna!" called Daltec.

Whhhhssshhh!

The arrow flew straight and true. Her heart leapt. But at the last moment, Krokol shifted his weight. *Clang!* The arrow glanced off his shoulder plate and flew on into the night, disappearing through the caved-in ceiling. She couldn't see where it landed.

Elenna clenched a fist in frustration. *So close…*

"Look!" gasped Daltec, suddenly.

She followed his pointing finger and spotted Ria. She had climbed to the top of a tower that rose from one corner of the hall. The pirate stood on the ramparts, exposed to the black sky, raising a silver staff over her head.

"It's a lightning staff," said Daltec. He had gone very pale. "Ria must be trying to summon a thunderstorm. Then she can create a lightning path, straight from here to Avantia."

Elenna's mouth went dry as she

understood. "She's going to take Krokol to Avantia," she muttered. "Straight to the heart of our kingdom…" *So instead of protecting the kingdom, the Master of the Beasts will destroy it!*

As they watched, Ria closed her eyes and lifted her head. She began to chant words in a strange, musical language that Elenna had never heard before.

Then a movement from Krokol drew all her attention. The Beast had picked up a massive chunk of rubble, twice the size of Elenna. Drawing back his cracked, ash-grey lips, Krokol sneered. Then with a grunt, he hurled the boulder.

"Look out!" yelled Elenna. She threw herself to one side. *CRRAAAASH!* The rubble exploded against the wall behind her. Dust rose, as Elenna rolled and sprang to her feet.

Krokol was already hefting another broken bit of masonry. He tossed it at Daltec, sending it skidding across the floor and forcing the wizard to hitch up his robes and dodge. *THUMP!* The rubble slammed against the wall.

Sooner or later, he's going to hit us...

"Through his legs!" yelled Elenna. "We've got to get to Ria."

Daltec looked terrified, but Elenna

grabbed him by the wrist and tugged him along.

Krokol watched with a leering grin as they darted in between his legs. *It's like he doesn't care*, thought Elenna, a leaden weight settling in her belly. *As though he knows he'll get us eventually...*

She shook off the thought and hurtled under the archway Ria had gone through. A spiral staircase led up inside the tower they'd seen from the hall. Elenna climbed it, two steps at a time. She could hear Daltec huffing and puffing after her.

They were halfway up when the whole staircase shook with a thunderous crashing sound. Elenna skidded to a halt.

"What was that?" yelped Daltec.

Then came a second crash, and a
massive grey fist smashed through

the wall in between Elenna and the wizard, scattering chunks of stone and dust in every direction.

"Daltec!" yelled Elenna. She tried to duck under Krokol's hand, but the Beast's fingers closed round her like iron bands. She caught a glimpse of Daltec's terror-stricken face. Then she was hauled out through the wall, held firmly in the grip of the Beast.

She gasped in the cold night air, as Krokol brought her closer to his face. She struggled, but with only her left arm free, she couldn't budge his grip at all.

She could smell the foul stench of the Beast's breath now. She could see the crooked stumps of his yellow teeth, and his long purple tongue, coiling and slathering his lips with saliva. *Is he going to eat me?*

"End it now!" Ria's voice called out in triumph. Elenna saw her out of the corner of her eye, leaning over the ramparts to watch. "Kill her, Krokol. Kill the little girl!"

THE LAST ARROW

Not this time, Krokol!

Elenna reached over her shoulder, and her fingers closed on the hilt of Tom's sword. With a grunt, she tugged it free.

Krokol's mouth was gaping wide. The tunnel of his throat disappeared into darkness ...

She slashed the sword down and

buried it deep in Krokol's hand. *Thunk!* Dark blood welled up around the cut, as thick as oil.

The Beast gave a growl of pain. For an instant, Elenna felt his grip lessen and she seized her chance, letting go of the sword hilt and heaving herself free. Down she went, plummeting towards the marble floor.

A sharp pain shot through her ankle as she landed, collapsing like a sack of turnips.

Elenna flexed her ankle and winced. But there was no time to examine it properly. Krokol tore the sword from his hand in a spray of blood, then hurled it away. His shadow fell over Elenna, and his dark eyes narrowed in fury.

Elenna lurched upright. She threw herself across the hall, half running, half hobbling. Pain shot through her ankle with every step, but she had to get to Ria before she opened the lightning path.

Glancing up, she was surprised to see that the pirate wasn't watching her any more. Instead, her attention was fixed on another figure, who had just appeared on the ramparts. *Daltec!*

Elenna managed a grim smile as she saw the wizard hurl a lump of rock at Ria, forcing her to dodge. *Who needs magic, anyway?* Daltec

lunged at Ria and snatched hold of
her staff. The pair of them struggled,
each trying to wrestle the magical

object away. As they fought, a red jewel fell from Ria's robes – it looked like Tom's ruby. *She must have stolen it from his belt to talk to the Beast. Maybe if I can get hold of it...*

Elenna had almost reached the bottom of the steps when something slammed into her shoulders and knocked her off her feet. Her knees smacked into the marble. She tried to stand, but found herself coated in a thick, dark slime that weighed her down, gluing her to the floor. It made her think of the black liquid King Jorah had drunk, when he'd first turned into Krokol.

Looking back, she saw the Beast with a hand outstretched, teeth bared in a savage smile. *He shot that slime at me*, Elenna realised. She could see strands of it dripping from his fingers. And now Krokol was advancing, claws flexing, as though he couldn't wait to tear her apart.

She scraped the black gunk from her clothes and staggered free. But when she reached for her bow, her blood ran cold…

It wasn't there.

Her eyes searched the room. Then she spotted it, lying on the floor close to the spot where she'd landed, when she tumbled from Krokol's grasp. *I must have dropped it when I fell*. Before she could dart over, Krokol's foot came down like a sledgehammer. *Crunch!* Elenna winced as she saw her wooden bow snapped clean in two beneath one of Krokol's talons.

No sword and no bow. Her fingers closed on the only weapon she had left – the last arrow, smeared with antidote. *If only I had something to fire it with...*

Krokol lowered his head and came at her, thundering across the marble like a charging bull.

Elenna whipped the arrow from the quiver as she turned and ran. She ducked through a side door, and found herself in the ruins of a grand atrium. Stone statues of armoured soldiers stood at intervals along the curving walls. The floor was a mosaic of tiles, chipped and faded, and in the centre of the atrium was a dried-up old fountain.

Crrrrassh!

Elenna spun round to see Krokol

ram his way through the wall,
showering the floor with rubble. He
flung out a claw, a string of thick
black slime spurting from his palm,
spattering the fountain right next to
where Elenna stood.

As fast as she could, Elenna

hobbled round, trying to put the fountain between her and Krokol. The Beast growled. Another gobbet of slime hurtled through the air, hitting a statue so hard that the head broke off and rolled across the tiled floor.

I can't keep this up... Her ankle stabbed at her every time she put weight on it. Krokol's bulk filled the atrium. If he didn't pin her in place with the black slime, he'd rip her apart with his claws. *I've got to fight back.*

She steeled herself, scanning the sinewy ash-grey body of the Beast. He loomed over her, crouching and stalking forwards like a wolf with its prey. His limbs and torso were crusted with the strange black armour, but here and there, she could see his flesh between the plates. If she could just cut him with the arrowhead, maybe Aduro's magic would do its work...

Elenna took a deep breath. *It's now or never!* She ran straight towards Krokol, ignoring the searing pain in her ankle. Krokol grunted. He swung wildly, too high.

At the last minute Elenna dived, twisting as she threw herself between the Beast's legs. She flicked the arrow up, and the tip of it sliced neatly into a thin line of grey flesh, right between the Beast's shin plate and his foot.

She felt the arrowhead bite. Dark blood gushed across the mosaic, and Krokol hissed with pain.

Elenna came crashing down on her shoulder on the other side. She tried to stand, but her injured ankle gave way under her with a burst of agony. She thumped down on the floor again, helpless and groaning.

Krokol's shadow fell over her, and she turned her head to see him leering. He raised a fist for the killing blow. The claws glittered, each one as sharp as a spearhead.

What was I thinking? I've barely scratched him!

But Krokol hesitated. His fist

trembled. Then, to Elenna's shock, he began to lower it. He shook his huge head, as though dazed. He stumbled, almost crushing her with one massive foot. He swayed... And Elenna realised with a lurch of her heart what was happening. *The antidote...it's working!*

The Beast lifted his foot again, ready to stamp down on Elenna. But his eyelids drooped and he staggered, crashing hard into the fountain. He clung to it for a moment. Then his body went limp, and he began to topple...

He's going to fall on top of me!

Drawing up the last ounce of her strength, Elenna threw herself into a roll to dodge Krokol. Her body smacked into the wall.

BOOOOM! The whole chamber shook with the impact as the Beast's body cracked the mosaic floor. Statues toppled and fell. Elenna's bones shuddered, and her teeth rattled.

Then at last there was silence.

Krokol lay utterly still, limbs spread out.

Slowly, cautiously, Elenna heaved herself towards the body. She saw the Beast shift, and she froze. *He's waking up...* Then she saw that he wasn't moving at all. *He's shrinking!*

Krokol's armour was fading, disappearing from his body.

Underneath it, his grey flesh was transforming as colour seeped into his skin. Last of all, the Beast's horrifying features rearranged themselves into a face that Elenna knew well. *Tom's face*.

Elenna hardly dared to breathe. Her friend was no longer a Beast. But his eyes were closed, and his chest wasn't moving at all.

Desperately, she fumbled for Tom's wrist. *No pulse either*.

She let out a long, shuddering breath. *He's dead*. She didn't want to believe it, but it was true. *I've killed him – my best friend. I've killed Tom!*

FOR AVANTIA

Tom blinked. He flexed his fingers.
He hardly dared to believe it. *I'm
in control... Ria's enchantment is
broken. I'm me again!*

He was lying on the cold floor. He
turned his head and saw Elenna
crouched over him.

"Elenna," he said.

But something was wrong. She

didn't seem to hear him. Her mouth was moving, but he couldn't hear any sound coming out. Her skin was slightly transparent too, and he realised he could see straight through her. *What's going on?*

"I'm right here!" he said, sitting up. "I'm fine!"

He sat up and gazed around, and to his surprise he realised the ruined atrium was gone. It looked brand new, the stone statues brightly painted and the mosaic floor was unbroken. The fountain ran with sparkling clear water, and the vaulted ceiling was painted with golden birds. As he stood up, Elenna remained on the ground, still bent over a ghostly corpse. *It's me!*

"Where am I?" he mumbled to himself. He saw his red jewel on the floor and snatched it up, inserting it into his belt. He couldn't see Ria anywhere. Then a movement caught

his eye, and he gasped.

Krokol was standing at the other side of the room, over a ghostly form of himself. The solid Beast turned his black eyes on Tom, and his tongue lashed between his savage teeth. *Now we will fight*, said a voice in Tom's head. *Here in this world, to see who has the right to live.*

Tom crouched, raising his fists to fight. The Beast was much bigger than him, and he didn't have his sword or shield.

"I'll defeat you, Krokol," Tom said, calmly. "While there's still blood in my veins."

You? the voice snarled inside

Tom's head. *You're just a boy!*

The Beast flexed his claws, sizing Tom up. *Even Tanner could not defeat me*, taunted Krokol. *And he was one of the greatest warriors ever to walk your wretched kingdom.*

Before Tom could react, the Beast launched himself forward and swung a fist. *THUMP!* It smacked into Tom's stomach.

"Oof!" Tom grunted as he was thrown backwards, all the way across the atrium, his head slamming against the wall. He staggered, seeing stars.

Krokol's grey lips split in a cruel grin. He stepped closer, raising his other fist...

"Halt!"

Tom turned at the sudden cry.

Standing in the archway was a man dressed in a leather jerkin, well built, with square shoulders and a shaggy grey beard.

Tom blinked, hardly able to believe his eyes. His head ached, but he wasn't seeing things. He'd only met Tanner a few times, but had seen countless pictures in the library scrolls and on tapestries, and he'd heard the first hero described in poems and songs...

"Tanner!" he cried.

The famous warrior stepped into the atrium. "I've waited nearly four hundred years for this," he said. His voice was low and gruff. "My sword was destined to slay Krokol. But I never guessed it would be another who would wield it."

I smashed your blade, snarled Krokol's voice. *I broke it to pieces!*

Tanner turned his icy gaze on the Beast. "Did you?" he asked.

He lifted his hand. Tom saw that it held a sword hilt, with only a broken stub of blade sticking out. But as he watched, glowing shards of steel began to appear out of thin air and join together, one by one, until Tanner held a complete sword in his hand, the shining blade bright and keen.

The old warrior locked eyes with Tom. "For Avantia," he murmured. Then his fist flew open, and the sword vanished.

Tom gasped. His fingers were clenched around something, and he saw that he now held Tanner's sword in both hands.

Krokol snorted with rage. *Little boy! You dare try to defeat me?*

Tom whirled round, just in time to see Krokol fling out a hand. A blast of black slime spurted from his palm. Tom tried to dodge it, but he felt the slime thump wetly against his wrists. He tugged hard, but the slime had glued his hands to the sword hilt.

Whumph! A second gout of slime

spattered against Tom's chest. Then he was heaved off his feet, tumbling to the floor. Glancing up, he saw that the slime stretched all the way

back to Krokol's hand. The Beast was reeling him in, like a fisherman with a net.

Tom struggled, but it was no good. He was dragged helplessly across the floor.

Krokol let out a barking noise that might have been a laugh. *In a moment you'll be mine*, hissed his voice. *Then I'll return to life...and I'll kill the little girl, too!*

A NEW POWER

Got to...get...free... thought Tom.

He tried to draw on the power of the golden breastplate. But no matter how hard he concentrated, he couldn't feel its magical strength flooding into his limbs. *Wherever I am, the Golden Armour doesn't work here.*

He scraped across the tiles, as

Krokol pulled him closer. He tried to brace his boots against the floor, but it was impossible to get a grip.

Krokol threw out his other hand, and another string of sticky slime smacked into Tom's ankles, gluing them together. His hands and feet were useless. There was no escape.

"Don't give up." It was Tanner who spoke, though Tom couldn't see him from the floor. His voice was calm and steady, and it made Tom feel calmer too. "Remember, you are not Master of the Beasts because you are strong, or because you have magic."

"Why, then?" grunted Tom. He struggled against the slime, but it

held him firm.

"Because of your heart," said Tanner. "That is why you have always completed your Quests. Be at peace. Be focused. The path to victory will reveal itself, even in the jaws of defeat."

Tom nodded. He closed his eyes and let himself relax, even as Krokol dragged him in. *How can I get out of this?* He couldn't move his hands or legs. He couldn't swing his sword.

But what if he could somehow use Krokol's own slime against him?

Coward! growled Krokol. *You would surrender so easily?*

In a moment, Krokol would be able to reach him. Tom let the

Beast pull him close. But at the last moment, he pushed off the ground with both feet. And this time, he drove himself *towards* the Beast.

Tom saw Krokol's eyes widen with shock. But it was too late. The Beast's slime was tugging Tom towards him, faster and faster. Krokol tried to get away, but the slime only pulled Tom with him. At the same moment, Tom angled the sword, pointing it like a lance at the Beast's chest, between the black plates of his armour.

Thump! The blade buried itself in Krokol's body, right up to the hilt.

The Beast gaped. His jaw fell open, and a whimper escaped. His teeth set in a grimace of rage. Tom clung on to

the sword hilt, caught for a moment in
a tight embrace with Krokol. He felt
the slime loosen, slipping away from
his hands and legs.

He shoved himself away, tugging the blade free and landing in a crouch on the floor. Krokol slumped forward, falling to his knees with a thump that made the ground shake. But he was still alive.

Not for long...

Tom drew the sword back and swung it straight at the Beast's neck, putting all his weight behind the blow.

He felt the metal meet the resistance of Krokol's flesh, then it sank straight through to the other side.

The Beast opened his mouth, as if to roar again. But instead his head toppled, rolled across the floor and came to rest at Tom's feet.

Without a sound, Krokol's body blurred at the edges then seemed to melt into black smoke. Tom coughed and spluttered as the ashy cloud passed over him and drifted up towards the sky above.

It's over...

It was Tom's turn to sink to his knees. His limbs felt suddenly heavy, his body drained of energy.

Now that Krokol was gone, his gaze fell on the ghostly form of Elenna again. She was kneeling on the ground, still looking at Tom's own body. Tears stained her cheeks as she shook her head. Daltec had joined her, one arm around his friend's shoulders.

Tom wanted to cry too. He turned to Tanner. "Am I dead?" he asked.

The old warrior smiled and shook his head. "Now that you have driven Krokol from the world, you will return to life. But you will not be the same."

Tom frowned, feeling uneasy. "What do you mean?"

"You will have a new power," said Tanner. "The power to call on your predecessors, just as you call on the Good Beasts, whenever you might need our help."

"Really?" Tom's heart soared. "Will you fight alongside me, then?"

"I wish we could," said Tanner,

sadly. "But we cannot truly return to the land of the living. What we can offer you is our wisdom and experience."

"I'm honoured," said Tom. "I hope I'll see you again, Tanner." Then another thought struck him, and he felt his heart racing. "What about my father? Can I call on Taladon?"

"We are all within your grasp," said Tanner. "Every Master and every Mistress of the Beasts."

With a twist of his gut, Tom realised that the image of Tanner was fading. The whole room was – darkness encroached like a sudden nightfall. "Don't go!" he cried. "Please... Tanner? Tanner!"

For a moment, all was black, and Tom felt weightless. Fear spiked in his heart. Perhaps it hadn't worked, after all. Perhaps he'd be stuck in limbo for ever...

"I can feel a pulse!" said Elenna's voice.

"His fingers moved!" Daltec exclaimed. "And his armour's changing!"

Tom opened his eyes to see his friends leaning over him, lips parted in shock.

I'm alive...

Tom hardly had time to be relieved before Elenna threw her arms around him, hugging and squeezing him so tight he could barely breathe. He realised the armour he wore was no longer black, but gold once again.

"We thought you were dead!" Elenna cried.

Tom grinned and hugged his friend back. "I think I almost was," he said. "But I'm back now."

"What a relief," muttered Daltec, mopping his brow with a sleeve. Then he seized Tom by the arm. "But there's no time to lose. Ria's trying to open a lightning path to Avantia!"

Tom gritted his teeth. "Leave it to me," he said. "I've a bone to pick with that pirate."

He lurched to his feet and dashed out of the atrium with Elenna and Daltec following behind.

Glancing around the huge ruined hall, Tom spotted Ria up on the ramparts, through the gaping hole in the ceiling. The sky above her was thick and dark with storm clouds, and her staff glowed bright white.

"Ah, my servant awakes!" said Ria, with a sneer. "I order you to kill Elenna, Tom. And make it quick!"

Tom shook his head. "I don't think so, Ria. Whatever spell you used on me, it's broken now. I'm taking you back to Avantia in chains."

Ria's lip curled. "So you've come to your senses…what little of them you had to begin with. Too bad! We could have done great things together, you and I. But don't worry, I'll return soon enough."

Throwing back her head, the pirate howled a string of strange words up at the sky. Then there was a blinding white flash of lightning. It struck her staff, and for an instant Ria glowed like the sun. But when Tom blinked and looked again, she was gone.

He clenched his fists with frustration. "If we'd got here a little sooner…"

"You did all you could, Tom," said Elenna, gently. Tom saw that she was staring at the floor, unable to meet his gaze. "I…er…hope you can forgive me," she muttered.

"Forgive you?" Tom grinned. "I was the one who turned into a horrifying Beast. I should ask you to forgive me!"

A smile crept across Elenna's face.

"Well, I did sort of kill you…" she said. "Call it even?"

Tom laughed. "Agreed."

After so many Quests together, Tom knew that Elenna would always do the right thing – even if it meant standing up to him. *No matter what happens, we'll always be friends*, he thought. He stepped forward and hugged her tightly.

"I'm just glad you're back," said Elenna, her voice trembling with relief.

"Ahem," said Daltec, hovering awkwardly. "What about Ria? Should we follow her?"

Tom and Elenna broke apart.

"What do you think?" said Elenna.

Tom shook his head. "She won't
risk attacking Avantia without
Krokol to back her up," he said. "And
if I know her, the next thing she'll do
is sulk for a while."

Elenna grinned. "I suppose the kingdoms are safe from her scheming then. For now, anyway."

They began to walk through the ruined hall, picking their way among the rubble that had been hurled by Krokol in the fight.

Now that the Quest was finally over, Tom's body ached with tiredness. "I can't wait to get back," he said. "I'm going to sleep for a week!"

"I'll sleep for a month!" said Elenna. "Questing alone is hard work. Especially when the Beast at the end of it is your best friend."

"I'm sure you can have all the sleep you want," said Daltec. "After the feast, of course."

Tom's heart sank. "Feast?"

"Oh yes," said Daltec. "King Hugo will certainly want to hold one in your honour. There'll be ten courses, at least. Jugglers too, I expect, and minstrels. All for you two! Goodness me, I can't wait…"

As the wizard walked on, still talking, Elenna rolled her eyes at Tom. He stifled a smile. *Elenna hates being the centre of attention almost as much as I do!*

Even so, he felt sure they could put up with it for one evening. *It's a small price to pay*, he thought, *so long as Avantia is safe.*

THE END

1

CONGRATULATIONS, YOU HAVE COMPLETED THIS QUEST!

At the end of each chapter you were
awarded a special gold coin
The QUEST in this book was
worth an amazing 8 coins.

Look at the Beast Quest totem picture
opposite to see how far you've come
in your journey to become

MASTER OF THE BEASTS.

The more books you read,
the more coins you will collect!

Do you want your own
Beast Quest Totem?
1. Cut out and collect the coin below
2. Go to the Beast Quest website
3. Download and print out your totem
4. Add your coin to the totem

www.beastquest.co.uk

READ THE BOOKS, COLLECT THE COINS!
EARN COINS FOR EVERY CHAPTER YOU READ!

550+ COINS
MASTER OF THE BEASTS

550+
515
480
445
410
395
380
365
350
320
290
260
230
217
206
191
180
146
112
78
44
30
19
8

410 COINS
HERO

350 COINS
WARRIOR

230 COINS
KNIGHT

180 COINS
SQUIRE

44 COINS
PAGE

8 COINS
APPRENTICE

READ ALL THE BOOKS IN SERIES 24:
BLOOD OF THE BEAST!

BeastQuest
NEW BLOOD
ADAM BLADE

Meet three new heroes with the power to tame the Beasts!

Amy, Charlie and Sam – three children
from our world – are about to discover the
powerful legacy that binds them together.

They are descendants of the *Guardians of
Avantia*, an elite group of heroes trained by
Tom himself.

Now the time has come for a new generation
to unlock the power of the Beasts and
fulfil their destiny.

*Read on for a sneak peek at how the
Guardians first left Avantia by magic...*

Karita of Banquise gazed in
awe at Tom, Avantia's mighty,
bearded Master of the Beasts.

Under his leadership, she and her
companions would today face their
greatest challenge.

Tom pointed towards the brooding
Gorgonian castle. "We must recover
the chest of Beast Eggs Malvel
stole," he reminded them. His fierce
blue eyes moved from Karita to the
others. Dell of Stonewin, whose
bloodline connected him to Beasts of
Fire; Fern of Errinel, linked to Storm
Beasts; Gustus of Colton, bonded
with Water Beasts.

Malvel will be expecting an attack," Tom said. "His power is lessened, but he is still formidable." His eyes locked on Karita. "Stealth will be our greatest ally."

Karita felt as though her whole life had been a preparation for this moment. Countless hours spent studying the ancient tomes, day after day of gruelling combat training, months learning how to influence the will of Stealth Beasts and control the powers that filled the Arcane Band at her wrist.

But was she ready?

She gazed into Tom's face, and her doubts faded.

Yes!

A low rumble came from the

castle. Flashes of green lightning shot from the clouds as a swarm of screeching creatures erupted from the battlements.

Karita shuddered as Malvel's hideous minions streaked through the sky. They were man-sized, with white hides, limbs tipped with hooked claws and gaping jaws lined with sharp teeth. Their leathery wings cracked like whips.

"Karrakhs!" muttered Tom. "Karita – go!"

She nodded and slipped away behind jagged rocks. She turned to see the swarm of foul creatures engulf her companions. Tom's sword flashed. Howls rang out from the Karrakhs. The Guardians were using their Arcane Bands to form weapons that spun and slashed!

Karita raced for the castle, keeping low behind the ridge of rocks. Reaching the walls, she climbed up a gnarled vine and found a narrow window to crawl through. She looked back again. Tom and the Guardians had battled their way through the castle gates.

Well fought!

She dropped into a room and crept to the door. Torches burned in the corridor, casting shadows. The castle was silent, but Karita felt a growing dread as she slipped along the walls.

She knew where the chest of Beast eggs was hidden. But would Malvel allow her to get to them?

She came to a circular room, and saw the chest standing by the wall. Her heart hammering, Karita opened the lid and gazed down at the eggs. They were different sizes, shapes and colours. One slipped from the pile and she caught it in her gloved hand. It was pale blue, about the size of a goose egg. Acting on instinct, she slipped it inside her breastplate.

Crash!

She spun around. Malvel stood against the room's closed door.

"Did you really think you could enter my domain unseen?" he snarled, a green glow igniting in his palm. His voice was weaker than she'd imagined. "I *wanted* you to come here. After all, only a Guardian can hatch a Beast Egg."

Karita swallowed hard, seeking a way to escape.

"You and your friends will hatch these Beasts and I will drink in their power," growled the wizard. "I will become mighty again and Avantia will bow before me!"

"I'm not afraid of you!" Karita shouted.

A ball of green fire exploded from Malvel's hand. Karita dived aside, seared by the heat.

She leaped up, thrusting her right arm towards the wizard. The Arcane Band began to form a weapon, but another blast of fire sent her sliding across the floor.

Malvel loomed over her, both hands

burning green. Before he could strike, the door burst open and Tom and the Guardians rushed into the room.

"No!" roared Malvel. "Where are my Karrakhs?"

"Defeated!" shouted Tom, whirling his sword to deflect Malvel's green flames. "Guardians! Take the eggs!"

Look out for
Beast Quest: New Blood
to find out what happens next!

Beast Quest

ULTIMATE HEROES

Find out more about
the NEW mobile game at
www.beast-quest.com